USBORNE HOTSHOTS
GHOSTS

USBORNE HOTSHOTS
GHOSTS

Caroline Young
Consultant: Tim Dedopulos BSc

Edited by Cheryl Evans
Designed by Karen Tomlins

Illustrated by Graham Humphreys

Series editor: Judy Tatchell
Series designer: Ruth Russell

Additional material by
Lynn Myring,
Christopher Maynard
and Eric Maple

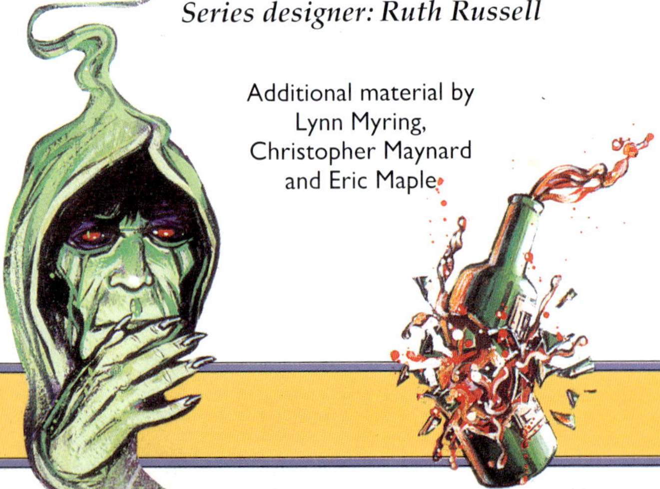

CONTENTS

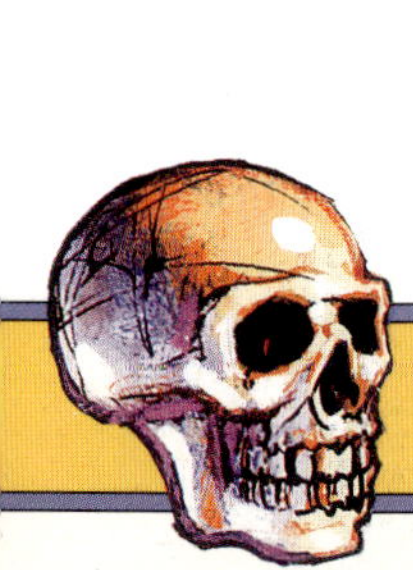

What is a ghost?

A ghost is usually thought to be the spirit of a dead person, supposed to haunt living people as a pale or shadowy vision. Not everyone becomes a ghost, not everyone can see ghosts and by no means everyone believes in them. But those who do say there are lots of different types of ghosts, with a wide variety of reasons for lingering in this world. Here are some of the most common kinds.

Haunting ghosts

Some restless spirits forlornly haunt the place where they once lived, or died. Often, something very unpleasant, such as murder, happened to them on that spot and they seem to relive their last moments there forever because they were so shocking.

Spirits with a message

A few ghostly visitors seem to have a message they feel they must deliver, usually to someone they knew well. In one strange case in the 18th century, a Dutch widow was visited by a ghost who said her dead husband had owed him 25,000 Dutch guilders. Then the ghost of her husband came and told her where to find proof that the debt had been paid and the money was not owed at all.

Ghosts of the living?

There are many stories of visits from ghosts of people before they have died. For example, soldiers badly wounded on a battlefield sometimes visit friends and relatives in spirit before they die, as if to say farewell. Another sort of living ghost is your own ghostly self. Some people claim to have seen

this uncanny sight, which is thought to be a bad omen. The English poet Shelley saw his double, or *doppelganger* as it is called, in 1822 while living by the sea in Italy. Within weeks he drowned.

Poltergeists

Where a poltergeist is at work, furniture flies around, invisible hands may pinch or tug hair and people have even been thrown into the air. These weird things usually happen around young people. Some experts think it has to do with the energy in their changing bodies as they grow up, which provides the power for poltergeist activity. If they are right, then poltergeists are not really ghosts at all.

Around the world

The tradition of ghost stories is much the same all over the globe. Most people seem to be chilled by the thought of restless spirits, but sometimes a ghost is said to help or comfort someone. In some countries, the spirit world is seen as a natural part of everyday life, or religion.

Haunted houses

Some of the most famous places to be haunted by ghosts are houses. Here you can find out about some of the strange things that are likely to occur in a haunted house.

Things to look out for in a haunted house

Hidden bones may suggest a violent death in the house.

Mysterious footprints appear of their own accord.

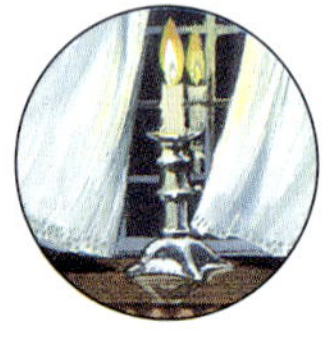

Doors and windows open and close themselves for no reason.

Eerie thumps and crashes are heard in empty rooms.

Walking through walls

In an old house, the layout of the rooms may have changed several times over the years. Doorways are blocked off and new walls built.

Ghosts continue to follow the routes they used when they were alive, ignoring more recent walls and stairs and so on.

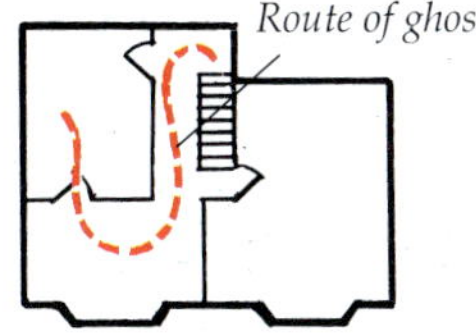

Floor plan of house 1896

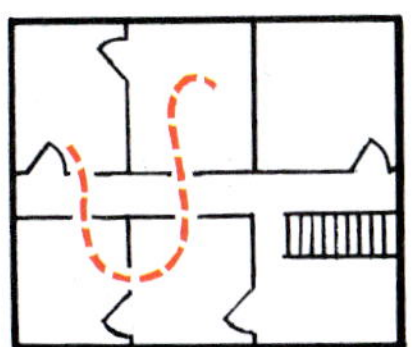

Floor plan of offices 1996

The Amityville hauntings

One house that fairly recently experienced many of these phenomena was not even very old. The house in Amityville, near New York, USA, was the scene of a multiple murder. Ronald DeFeo shot dead his brothers, sisters and parents.

Brave new occupants

The Lutz family moved into the house after DeFeo's trial but were soon spooked by windows and doors that opened on their own, red eyes glowing in the dark and cloven footprints in the snow outside.

Quick exit

When green slime began oozing down the walls they knew they had to leave. The Lutzes made lots of money from telling the story of their stay in Amityville and experts now think the effects may all have been faked – but nobody knows for sure.

There may be bloodstains that no scrubbing can remove.

A ghostly figure may glide from room to room through walls.

If a clock strikes thirteen, you can be sure there is a ghost around.

Ghostly hands may play a creepy melody on an old piano.

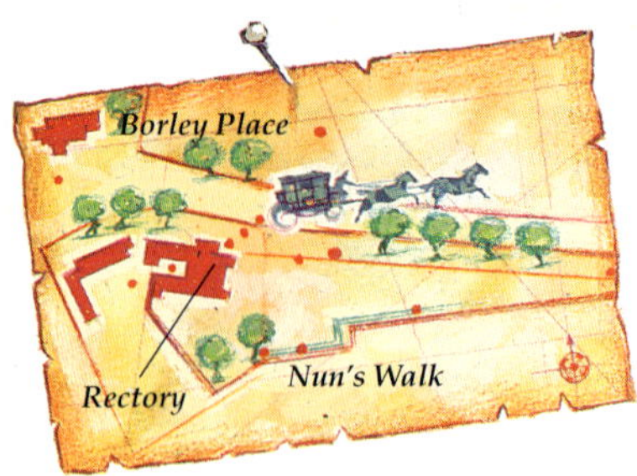

This is a plan of the grounds of Borley Rectory.

Ghostly nun

People who lived there were frequently startled by the shadowy face of a nun peering through the windows. A path in the garden was known as the Nun's Walk because her lonely figure was often seen scurrying along it. Nobody knows what tragic story kept her there, though some believe she was punished for trying to elope with a monk.

Borley Rectory

Borley Rectory stood on a lonely spot in Suffolk, England. Until it was destroyed by fire in 1939, it was often called "the most haunted house in England".

Grieving nun?

Where was this coach going?

Spectral coach

Several occupants of Borley reported a phantom black coach speeding silently through the Rectory gates. Others spoke of stones flying through the windows, ghostly bell ringing, and phantom footsteps.

Borley Rectory is a ruin today, but you can still visit it and try to catch a glimpse of its ghostly former inhabitants.

Winchester Mystery House

The wealthy American Winchester family made rifles. When Sara Winchester's husband died, she said that spirits had told her to build a home for all the ghosts of people killed by the rifles.

Amazing maze

Sara said the spirits' building instructions kept changing and the house became a giant maze: stairs led nowhere, doors opened into thin air and rooms were walled shut.

Lonely banquets

Sara held banquets in the house for ghostly guests only she could see and slept in a different bedroom each night. Today, the Winchester Mystery House is a great tourist attraction.

Phantoms of the high seas

Sailors have always spun yarns about ghostly warnings and strange happenings at sea. Perhaps it is the daily dangers of their life at the mercy of the mighty and unpredictable oceans that make them superstitious.

This ghost ship is called the Libera Nos.

Sailors say that the ghost ship's hull is painted bright yellow.

The Libera Nos

Sailors crossing the Pacific Ocean dread seeing the ghost ship Libera Nos. They say disaster follows those who glimpse it, bathed in an eerie light, with its crew of skeletons.

Some sailors say they see the skeleton captain holding up an hourglass and a telescope.

The Libera Nos' captain forced his petrified crew to sail on through a terrible storm in 1871. When a glowing shape appeared in the captain's cabin to warn him to turn back, he scorned it, then shot at it with his pistol. The strange being cursed the captain and his crew to sail the seas for all eternity. Any ship that crossed their path was also doomed, it said.

Over the last century, several ships have reported seeing the ghostly Libera Nos. Sailors say the glowing ship disappears as soon as it has passed them. Tragedy has followed these sightings in almost every case.

The Great Eastern

In 1858, the Great Eastern was the largest passenger ship in the world. Yet, from the start, she was jinxed. Some workers were killed while building her, and one vanished. On her first trip a funnel blew up, killing six people, and her paddle wheels were torn off in a storm.

Passengers complained of a hammering from below, but nobody was working there. When the ship was scrapped in 1885, a skeleton was found in the hull. Was this the missing shipbuilder – could it have been his ghostly hammering that passengers heard?

Mary Celeste

On November 4th 1872, the Mary Celeste sailed out of New York for Genoa, Italy. Captain Briggs, his wife, daughter and eight crew were on board. On November 25th, Briggs logged the ship's exact position – the last entry in the ship's log.

Vanishing crew

Ten days later, another ship, the Dei Gratia, saw the Mary Celeste drifting and three sailors boarded her.

They found uneaten breakfast on the table, but not a soul anywhere and no clue as to why, or where, they had gone.

Cursed ship

A public investigation failed to prove what had happened on the Mary Celeste. Although the ship was sold, sailors would not sail on her, believing her cursed.

The Flying Dutchman

Probably the most famous phantom ship is The Flying Dutchman, often seen off The Cape of Good Hope, South Africa.

Sailors say disaster follows the appearance of the ghostly sailing ship.

The ship's captain refused to head for port during a violent storm off the Cape, the unlucky ship sank and all aboard perished.

Pirate ghost

When most goods were carried by ship, pirates roamed the seas trying to steal them. The famous pirate, Captain Kidd, was captured and sentenced to death in 1701. He was hanged, then his dead body was put on display as a warning to other pirates. His ghost is still said to be seeking plunder off the coast of New England, USA.

Captain Kidd's body on display in a gibbet.

Ship in trouble

In 1959, two British naval ships went to the rescue of a landing craft in distress off the coast of Devon. When they drew near the craft, which was flying the flag of the Second World War Free French navy, it vanished.

The haunted submarine

The German World War I submarine, UB65, seemed doomed. Several people were killed during its construction, and dreadful things happened on board from the start.

A series of disasters

Among other things, the sailors were nearly suffocated by fumes from the submarine's batteries; more people were killed when a torpedo exploded while being loaded; and the ghost of one of the officers killed in this explosion began to be seen on board. Late in the war, an American ship found the UB65 drifting at sea. Suddenly, it exploded and sank.

As it slid under the water for the last time, the American sailors saw the ghostly officer appear once more.

Noisy ghosts

Poltergeists can be a real nuisance and very often make life a misery for the young person around whom their activity focuses. Many of those who suffer the torments of these noisy ghosts are never really the same again.

Trouble in Turin

In a bar in Turin, Italy, in 1900, strange noises began to disturb customers. Every night there came the sound of smashing bottles in the cellar, scaring people off. A ghost expert saw furniture, clothes and shoes flying around and diagnosed a poltergeist. He said the only way to stop it was to fire the young waiter who worked there.

After the waiter was fired, the smashing stopped.

Amherst evil

A poltergeist made life misery for a family in Amherst, Canada in 1889. Trouble began when Esther Cox, who was only seventeen, heard strange noises under her bed. The noises became deafening knocks and one night Esther swelled up like a balloon and her hair stood on end. Threatening messages appeared on her bedroom walls and flaming matches dropped onto Esther's bed. Esther fell ill and left the house. When she returned, the dreadful happenings gradually stopped.

The Bell Witch

In 1817, "something" began haunting the Bell family in Robertson County, Tennessee, USA. Whatever it was, it pulled off the family's bedclothes, slapped their faces and filled the house with shrieks and whistles. They called it the Bell Witch.

When Mr. Bell died suddenly in 1820, the witch announced that she had poisoned him. They later found a mysterious bottle containing liquid, a few drops of which killed their cat.

The witch vanished, promising to return in seven years. She has never done so... yet.

Alien force

A Brazilian family was plagued by a poltergeist in 1972. The Riberios were in their apartment when furniture began to fly around the room. A brick hit Mr. Riberio on the head and "something" grabbed a boiling kettle from his daughter, scalding her. Ghost experts could offer no solutions and the desperate family fled. Some say the poltergeist followed.

Spooky castles

Historic events, many of them dramatic and violent, often happen within castle walls and several phantom visitors may collect over the course of centuries. That's why castles are always a rich source of ghost stories.

Glamis castle

Glamis Castle in northern Scotland is said to be the home of ten ghosts. One is a phantom woman with no tongue. She has been seen running across the park screaming and pointing to her bleeding mouth.

Crathes Castle

Another spooky Scottish castle is Crathes near Aberdeen. Over the centuries there have been many reports of a ghostly woman who creeps across one of the rooms. She wears green and plucks a phantom baby out of the fireplace. Some years ago, the bones of a woman and child were discovered buried under the fireplace.

French phantoms

France is full of *chateaux*, or castles, many of which have ghostly inmates.

Revenge at Clisson

Jeanne de Clisson's husband was beheaded as a traitor by King Philippe IV of France. In revenge, Jeanne took to the seas with three ships and for thirteen years raided the king's ships and killed his men. Her reign of terror ended once the king and his family were dead, but her spirit still paces the battlements at Clisson Castle.

Blandy

At Blandy, near Paris, spooks are said to fly around the chateau each November 1st. A former lord of Blandy has also been seen, dressed for battle and on a white horse.

Unhappy Queen?

Versailles, south of Paris, is the site of a luxurious palace built by the French King Louis XIV in the 1700s. He and his wife, Marie Antoinette, went there often, until they were both beheaded by Revolutionaries in 1793.

Into the past

In 1901, two women heading for the Queen's small palace, the Petit Trianon, in the gardens of Versailles, say they felt the whole garden become unreal. They saw strange people in historic clothes, including a lady, sketching.

A familiar face

The two women recognized the sketcher from portraits of Marie Antoinette. They firmly believed they had seen the tragic Queen's ghost.

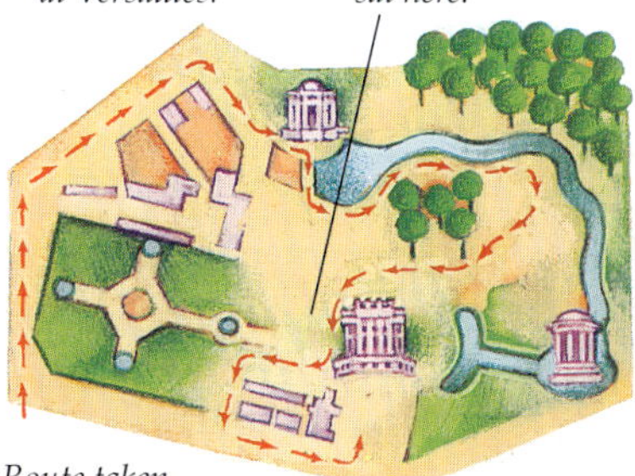

Plan of the gardens at Versailles.

The sketcher sat here.

Route taken by the two women.

The Tower of London

The gloomy Tower of London has witnessed thousands of gruesome deaths. It was used as a prison and many enemies of the crown were thrown in there, never to emerge.

Foul murders

Among the most tragic phantoms of the Tower were two young princes with a claim to the English throne at the end of the fifteenth century. Rivals wanted the princes dead and in 1483 they were imprisoned, then murdered, in the Tower.

The killer was never known, but many suspected their uncle, Richard, who became king after their deaths.

In 1647, builders found two boys' skeletons. They were buried and the princes stopped haunting.

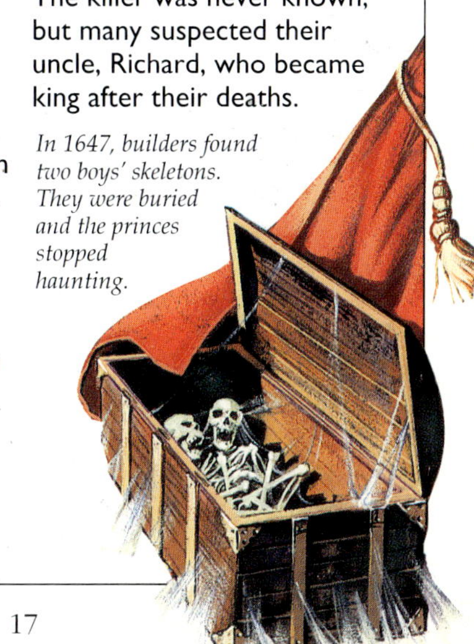

Spirits of famous people

Powerful and important people seem more likely to come to a traumatic end than most people. Not surprisingly, some of them seem to be unwilling to leave the places where they had such influence.

President Lincoln

American President Abraham Lincoln's spirit seems to have a very strong pull to stay in this world.

Frequent visitor

Lincoln was shot dead in 1865. Since then, his ghost has been seen in many rooms in the President's residence, the White House. Important guest, Queen Wilhelmina of the Netherlands, saw him in 1943.

Ghost train

The President's funeral train is said to haunt the route it took through New York State with his body. A skeleton band of musicians is seen on the train as it sweeps through stations, causing clocks to stop.

Napoleon's ghost

French Emperor, Napoleon Bonaparte was very powerful, but by 1821, his ambitious plans in ruins, he was exiled to the remote island of St. Helena.

On May 5th a tall man, his face barely visible beneath a dark hat and cloak, came to see Napoleon's mother who lived in Rome.

He told her that her son had died that day. She was puzzled, as news could not travel from St. Helena so fast then.

Months later, confirmation came that her son had died on May 5th. It dawned on her that his spirit had visited her on that day.

The wives of Henry VIII

Henry VIII had six wives, most of whom came to a sticky end. Three of them continue to haunt Henry's palace outside London, Hampton Court.

Sad mother

Jane Seymour, who died soon after the birth of Henry's son, Edward, glides around dressed in white, carrying a lit candle.

Desperate run

Henry's fifth wife, Catherine Howard, was imprisoned at Hampton Court before being beheaded at Henry's command. One night, she ran to the palace chapel where Henry was praying to plead for her life.

Henry would not talk to her and she failed to save her head, but her ghost still makes this last desperate run through the corridors.

Lady of the house

Anne Boleyn, who was also beheaded, is often seen in the palace's rooms and grounds. If you visit the palace, the map below shows you some good ghost-spotting places there.

Anne Boleyn, second wife

The ghost of Jane Seymour, third wife, is dressed in white. She carries a candle.

Poor Catherine Howard screams as she runs.

Anne Boleyn's ghost has been seen here, dressed in blue.

Catherine Howard runs down this corridor.

Jane Seymour's ghost comes out of this door.

Fantastic animals

It seems that animals can become ghosts, too, if you believe all the stories about them.

Black dogs

Stories of phantom black dogs come from many countries. One of the best-known is a British tale. This black dog had for centuries appeared whenever a member of the Vaughn family was about to die.

One Mr. Vaughn did not tell his wife the family tradition in case it scared her.

Dog of doom

One of their children fell ill and one day, after visiting the sick room, Mrs. Vaughn came shrieking downstairs, begging her husband to get rid of the black dog sitting on the child's bed. Mr. Vaughn raced up the stairs, but it was too late. As he had feared, the child was dead and the grisly black dog long gone.

Monster cat

In 1968, Margaret O'Brien bought an old house in Killakee, Southern Ireland. One evening, she was horrified to see a black cat as big as a dog in her hallway. She heard a deep voice say, "You cannot see me. You do not even know who I am."

Exorcism

Margaret finally asked a priest to exorcise the cat in a religious ceremony to rid the house of the phantom presence. Fortunately, it was a success and the cat was never seen again.

Runaway cattle

A cowboy in Texas, USA, once recklessly drove his cattle through a new ranch because it blocked his normal route. The herd stampeded and everyone on the ranch was killed.

The white tiger

Charles de Silva went hunting in the Indian jungle in the 1880s. As he stalked a tiger one night, a blind leper appeared before him. Just at that moment a tiger roared dangerously close to them. De Silva fled but heard the leper's screams as the tiger pounced.

De Silva fired, the leper's ghost rose before him and then tiger and leper both disappeared; but the son's face was scored by the tiger's claws and within a week he died of leprosy.

Man-eater

De Silva's servants warned him that the leper had been a sorceror and would take his revenge. He knew this was true when he heard of a man-eating tiger, white with leprosy, in the district.

Avenged

De Silva hunted the white tiger and shot him, but the terrible animal reappeared, poised to leap at de Silva's wife and son.

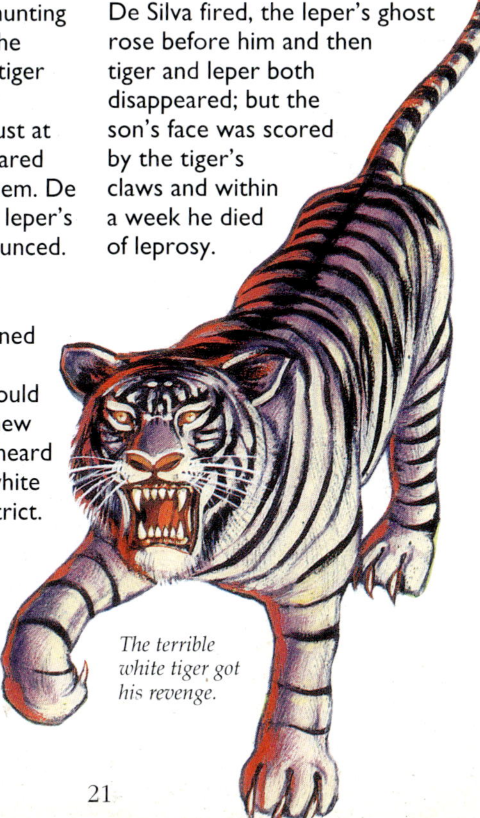

The terrible white tiger got his revenge.

Ghosts of war

Battlefields are places of noise, terror and death, so perhaps it's not surprising that those who die there return to haunt them. Battle ghosts almost always appear as complete armies, which is unusual, as most ghosts only haunt on their own. Oddly, phantom battles are often witnessed by more than one person at once, too.

Royal legend

According to legend, King Arthur, half-mythical king of sixth century Britain, is not dead, but simply sleeping. He will arise, with his Knights of the Round Table, to lead his people again in a moment of extreme danger in the future. The Knights, with Arthur at their head, are said to charge down Cadbury Hill, near Glastonbury, each Midsummer's Day, armed and ready for battle.

Viking raid

A thousand years ago, Vikings in longboats sailed the seas, coming ashore only to rob and wreck. Witnesses have seen a rerun of one Viking raid on the lonely Abbey of Iona, Scotland, which took place in the tenth century. Onlookers can even describe the scene in detail, saying how the Abbey burned and what the Vikings stole.

Noisy rerun

In 1951, two British women touring northern France were woken early one morning by the sound of gunfire and aircraft attacking. It started and stopped at the same times as a fierce battle in 1942 in nearby Dieppe. Did they witness an action replay?

Final defeat

A few weeks after Napoleon's final defeat at the Battle of Waterloo in June 1815, locals saw a ghostly re-enactment of the battle in the sky, with cavalry charging and guns firing.

Battle of Marathon

One of the earliest phantom battles was fought between Greeks and Persians at Marathon, in Ancient Greece. The apparitions were first seen soon after the Greek victory in the real battle in 490BC. People heard horses neighing and men fighting.

Edgehill replayed

One of the bloodiest battles of the English Civil War was at Edgehill in 1642. It was fought between the soldiers of King Charles I, called Cavaliers, and supporters of his opponent, Oliver Cromwell, who were known as Roundheads.

A few weeks after the battle, people spoke of seeing the terrible carnage being re-enacted by ghostly armies in the sky above the battleground.

Not long after, King Charles I sent some men to Edgehill to investigate. They saw the ghostly fighting, too, and even recognized one of the Cavalier princes.

For centuries, the battle was replayed, on each anniversary in October, and at Christmas. Recently, the recording seems faded, like a worn-out tape.

Ghosts of the East

There are ghost stories from all over the world. Here are some from Eastern countries.

The awful goryo

In Japan, an angry ghost seeking revenge is called a *goryo*. A Japanese peasant, Sogoro, became a *goryo* around 300 years ago, because he and his family were killed unjustly by their overlord. Sogoro had complained to his overlord's master, the shogun, about the heavy taxes and hard work of the peasants. Nobody was allowed to criticize a lord openly, so Sogoro was punished by death.

Revenge

As soon as Sogoro was dead, the overlord began to be troubled by nightmares, and his wife had terrible visions of Sogoro and his family dying.

Then, the overlord was arrested for corruption. In his prison cell, he begged the peasant's spirit for forgiveness. The farmers built a shrine to Sogoro, their hero, and at last the *goryo* left them in peace.

The ghostly wife

A Chinese man and his wife loved each other dearly. When the wife died, the husband broke

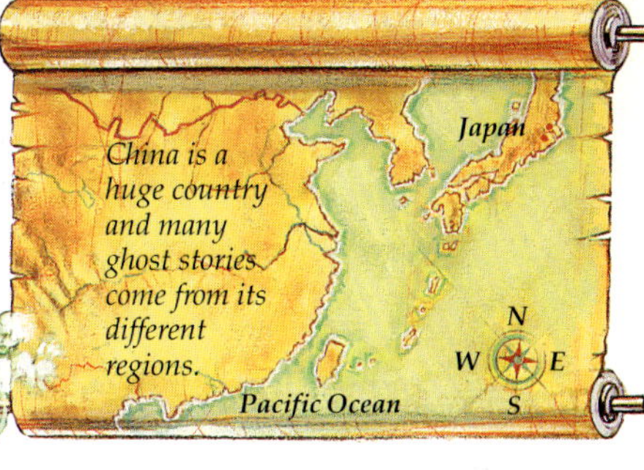

a coin in two and threw half into a well where ghosts were said to meet. He was told this would help him talk to his dead wife. He persuaded her spirit to come away with him, but when they reached a lonely farm, the wife went in to ask for a drink and never returned.

A long wait

Just then, the man heard a baby cry – the farmer's wife had just had a baby girl. Oddly, the baby would not open her right fist. The grieving husband stayed on the farm and on the girl's eighteenth birthday she at last opened her right hand to show the other half of the husband's coin. Reunited, the pair married again.

Tibetan tulpas

In Tibet, between China and India, people believe that spirits called *tulpas* can be brought to life by intense meditation. In the early 1900s, a French journalist, Alexandra David-Neel, meditated and created the *tulpa* of a fat monk. He was entertaining for a while, but soon became a nuisance. It took her six months to "think him away" again.

A host more ghosts

Here are some more creepy stories to chill your bones. The first two both involve travel, as many strange happenings seem to be associated with journeys.

Disappearing act

In this story, a man is driving on a rainy night in America. He sees a girl hitchhiking and picks her up. She is drenched so he lends her his jacket. When they reach the address she gives, she has vanished, with his jacket.

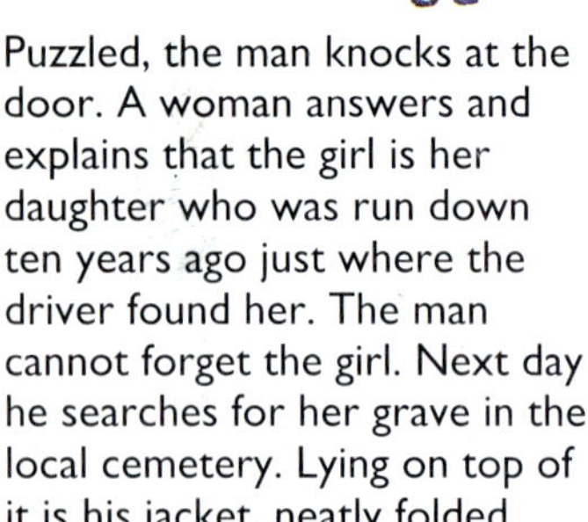

Puzzled, the man knocks at the door. A woman answers and explains that the girl is her daughter who was run down ten years ago just where the driver found her. The man cannot forget the girl. Next day he searches for her grave in the local cemetery. Lying on top of it is his jacket, neatly folded.

Tragic passenger

A British Colonel was sitting alone in a train compartment on a London to Carlisle train in about 1900. He awoke from a doze to find a young woman in black sitting opposite him, although it was impossible for anyone to have joined the train. The strange, sad woman stared silently at her lap.

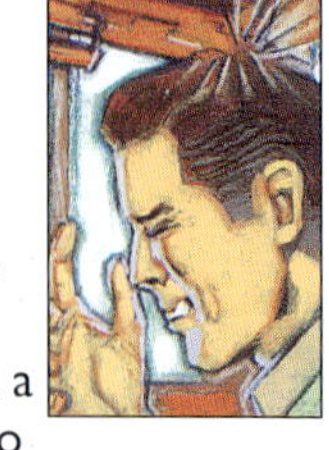

Suddenly the train braked and a falling suitcase knocked the Colonel out. When he awoke the woman had disappeared, but a porter knew who she was. Long ago, she and her husband were on the train and he leaned out of the window.

Horrifically, his head was severed and landed in his wife's lap. Her ghost relived this gruesome moment forever.

Mystery guest

At a party in Helsinki, Finland, in 1977, Pia Virtakallio saw a woman in outdated clothes come in from the freezing cold without a coat. Nobody else seemed to see her. Pia checked the guest list but there was nobody on it that she didn't know well. Years later, Pia read a book about an artist who had lived in that house. She was killed in an air raid in World War Two. Pia recognized the mystery guest from her picture.

The lady in black

A mournful widow in black is said to wander beside rivers in Mexico, weeping for her children. Once, she was infatuated by a young man and believed he would love her better without her children so she drowned them. Her black-clad spirit grieves on for her terrible deed.

Ghost to the rescue

In 1940, Patrick Thompson was working near Niagara Falls on the border between Canada and the United States. One night, he fell into the swirling waters by the falls and was drowned. Two years later, his son, Kenneth also slipped into the water. Unable to swim, he faced certain death. Then, he felt an invisible force and heard a voice guiding him to safety. The voice was his father's...

Ancient ghost story

This ghost story is 2,000 years old. There was a house in Athens that nobody could stay in because they were plagued by the ghost of an old man in chains. One day, a philosopher called Athenodorus moved in and, sure enough, began to hear ghostly moans and the phantom appeared. It led Athenodorus to a spot in the garden, to which it pointed pitifully. Next day, the authorities dug up the bones of an old man, chains still around his arms and legs. Once the body was properly buried, the ghost disturbed the house no longer.

In search of ghosts

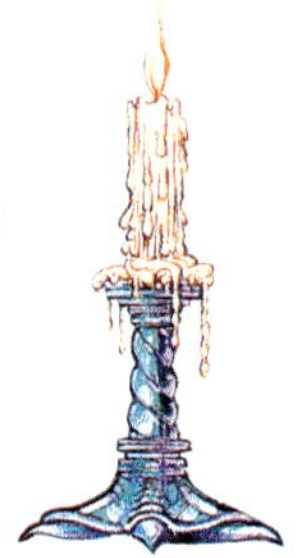

Whether or not you believe in ghosts, there are plenty of people who do. Some try to communicate with them and others try to find logical explanations for their existence. Here are some of the things that these people think, or believe.

Talking to ghosts

In Western countries, people called mediums claim they can talk to ghosts. Contacting dead friends and relatives through a medium was particularly popular in the 1900s.

At a gathering called a *seance* (pronounced say-onse), a medium goes into a kind of trance, then communicates messages from the spirits to people in the room.

Some mediums have been proved to be frauds, but not all...

Scientific explanations?

Modern theories of ghosts reject the idea that they are literally the spirits of people. Here is how some people explain ghosts.

Telepathy

Ghosts of living people are linked with telepathy – the ability to transfer thoughts to others. When the message is really strong, the receiver's

brain may interpret it as a visual image, or "ghost". For example, an Australian farmer had a ghostly visit from his wife while he was in a town far away. On his return, he found his wife had been killed at the exact moment he saw her. At the point of death is often a time when a ghost pays a call.

Fade away

Ghosts of the dead are thought to be the result of a violent event, such as a murder, which creates a force which imprints a "psychic image" where it occurs. The image stays by absorbing energy (such as heat) from the air. This is why ghosts are often associated with a chill feeling. It survives for many years but it fades over a very long time.

Fading woman

In one case, a spectral woman in a red dress was seen in the eighteenth century. Later she was seen in pink, then white. By 1939 just her footsteps were heard and in 1971 only her presence was felt by builders in the house.

Crash report

The airship R101 crashed in France in 1930. Two days later, its dead captain seemed to speak through a medium called Eileen Garrett. In the captain's voice, she described the crash with details only the captain could have known.

The fated airship crashed on its first flight.

Draw your own ghosts

If you enjoy ghost stories, you could make up some of your own, then illustrate them with your own drawings. Here are some ideas for how to do spooky effects.

Phantom ship

To draw this ship, dampen a sheet of paper with clean water. Dab runny poster or powder paints onto the sheet with a brush. The paint will spread and merge on the damp paper. Once the paint is dry, copy the ship with a grey felt-tip pen. Add foam by dabbing thick white paint around the ship with a rag or tissue.

This ship, The Palatine, was looted and set on fire in 1752. Its blazing ghost sails along the North American coast.

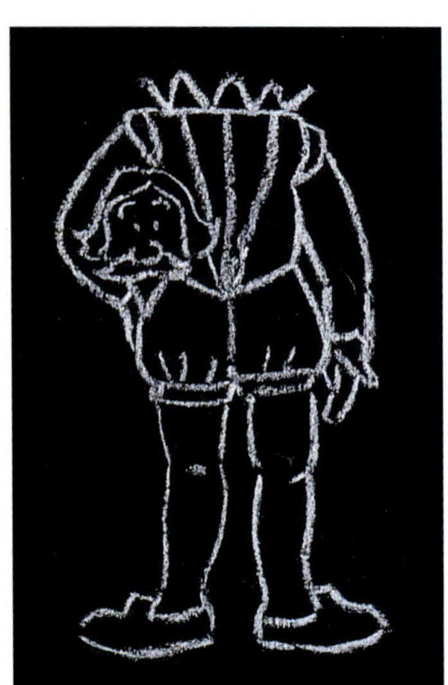

Headless ghost

Draw this headless historical ghost in white chalk on black paper for an eerie effect.

First draw a stick man like this on your paper in pencil. Draw the head about half as long as the body, and as if it is under his arm.

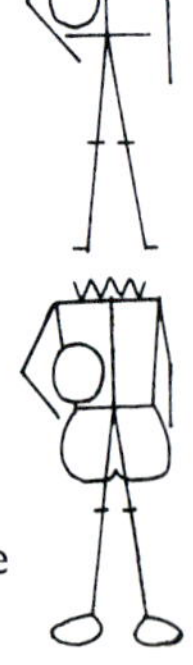

Join shoulders to waist. Add bloomers, a ruff, feet and other details (see left). Go over the outline in chalk. Smudge it with your finger.

Spooky graveyard

Rub a charcoal patch on white paper with a charcoal pencil or stick. Erase some shapes of gravestones, blades of grass and a ghost. Emphasize the rubbed out shapes and add details with charcoal lines, as in this picture.

See-through ghosts

Some ghosts seem to glide through solid objects. Here's a way to get a see-through effect.

1. Draw the outlines of a room or other background in pencil.
2. Draw your ghosts in the setting with a thin wax crayon.
3. Paint a thin layer of clean water over the whole picture. Add streaks of poster paint while the paper is still wet.
4. Once the paint is dry, go over your pencil outlines with a thin black felt-tip pen.

Ghostly shadows

These shadows have their own, creepy identity, separate from the person or thing they belong to. Copy these, or think up your own for a comic ghostly effect.

The clock's shadow looks like a monster's head.

Paint shadows dark blue.

This is like an evil spirit tapping someone's shoulder.

Shadows are longer and thinner than the original thing.

This shadow is a monster about to pounce.

Shadows join the feet, or base, of the person or thing.

Index

Additional illustrations by Elaine Lee, Seonaid Mackenzie,
Ray Jones, Oliver Frey, Rob McCaig, Sarah Simpson.

This book is based on material previously published in *The Usborne Book of the Haunted World*,
Usborne World of the Unknown – Ghosts and *The Usborne Guide to the Supernatural World*.